The Reactor

by J. Powell

illustrated by Paul Savage

Librarian Reviewer
Joanne Bongaarts
Educational Consultant
MS in Library Media Education, Minnesota State University, Mankato
Teacher and Media Specialist with Edina Public Schools, MN, 1993–2000

Reading Consultant
Elizabeth Stedem
Educator/Consultant, Colorado Springs, CO
MA in Elementary Education, University of Denver, CO

 STONE ARCH BOOKS
MINNEAPOLIS   SAN DIEGO

First published in the United States in 2007
by Stone Arch Books,
151 Good Counsel Drive, P.O. Box 669,
Mankato, Minnesota 56002.
www.stonearchbooks.com

Originally published in Great Britain in 2002
by Badger Publishing Ltd.

Original work copyright © 2002 Badger Publishing Ltd
Text copyright © 2002 Jillian Powell

The right of Jillian Powell to be identified as the author
of this work has been asserted by her in accordance
with the Copyright, Designs and Patent Act 1988.

Library of Congress Cataloging-in-Publication Data
Powell, Jillian.
    The Reactor / by J. Powell; illustrated by Paul Savage.
    p. cm. — (Keystone Books.)
    Summary: When Joe and his friends are locked out of an abandoned
building they have claimed as their own, they set out to discover whether
sinister activities are taking place there.
    ISBN-13: 978-1-59889-094-5 (hardcover)
    ISBN-10: 1-59889-094-8 (hardcover)
    ISBN-13: 978-1-59889-250-5 (paperback)
    ISBN-10: 1-59889-250-9 (paperback)
    [1. Cloning—Fiction.] I. Savage, Paul, 1971–, ill. II. Title.
PZ7.P87755Rd 2007
[Fic]—dc22   2006004059

1 2 3 4 5 6 11 10 09 08 07 06

Printed in the United States of America

Table of Contents

CHAPTER 1

The Staircase

"Me first," Joe said. "Count how many seconds to the bottom." The others stood aside.

The staircase curled below like an iron snake.

"Here goes!" Joe let out a battle cry.

Then he pushed off, sliding faster and faster, around and around.

"Five seconds!" Roy shouted.

The others followed, one after the other. They landed in a heap at the bottom.

"Awesome!" Joe said.

"Cool," Andrew said, nodding.

There was always something new to do in the Reactor. That was their name for it.

It was really just an old building, but people said there had been nuclear experiments there.

Joe came up with the name and it stuck. The Reactor was a great place.

The Reactor had long hallways where they could skateboard. It had dark, empty closets where they could hide things.

The hardest part was getting in, but they had mastered that. They knew all the secret entrances.

CHAPTER 2

Keep Out

"That's weird," Joe said. "There's a sign on the gate."

Joe and his friends were on their way to the Reactor.

"What does it say?" Doug asked.

"Keep Out," Joe read aloud.

"Look! There's barbed wire on top of the walls," Roy said as he pointed, "and the gates are locked."

Joe scrambled up on the gate.

"There's an old guy inside with a dog," he said. "He looks nasty."

"The guy or the dog?" Roy asked.

"Both," Joe said.

They hung around, wondering what to do.

"It's not fair," Doug said. "The Reactor is our place."

Just then the dog started barking inside the yard.

"Let's go around the back," Joe said. "We can try the other entrance."

It said "Keep Out" there, too.

They could hear someone inside the yard, with a dog on a chain.

"That's it, I guess," Roy said. He looked sad.

"What do we do now?" asked Doug.

"Wait," Joe said, "the bunker!"

The bunker was an old tunnel.

Its entrance was a manhole in the ground. It was covered with grass and leaves, and it was *outside* the fence.

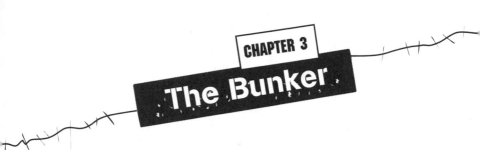

It was dark inside the bunker. It smelled like old shoes and stale air.

Joe felt around for the ladder that led into the Reactor.

"There it is!" Andrew said.

"Shhh!" Joe said.

They scrambled up the ladder one after the other. Soon they were inside a hallway that led to the labs.

"Smells like a hospital," Roy said, holding his breath.

They could hear voices coming from one of the labs.

They crept silently along the hallway, moving closer to the voices.

"Listen!" Joe said.

"She is aging faster than expected," a female voice said. "We need to keep an eye on her."

Andrew looked at Roy. "Who are they talking about?" he whispered.

"Must be a patient," Roy said. "It's a hospital, I bet. Look."

He had pushed one of the lab doors open. Inside, they could see rows of glass jars and trays that were marked with labels.

"Specimens," Roy said.

"Specimens of what?" Doug asked.

"Shhh!" Joe said. The voices were
gone. The meeting was ending.

Joe pushed the others through the open door. People were walking back to their labs. They wore white coats, like doctors.

Just then, Roy's watch began beeping. The footsteps outside slowed down.

"Did you hear something?" a voice asked.

Joe pushed the others inside one of the closets.

They heard the lab door creak open. A voice said something about a timer going off. Then the door slammed shut.

"That was close," Joe whispered.

Roy and the others were speechless.

Roy pointed to the shelf behind them.

In the dark, he could hardly make out what it was. He thought it looked like a tray of human ears.

CHAPTER 4

Lab Animals

"Joe!" Mr. Young's voice boomed across the classroom. "This is a math lesson, not an art lesson."

He held up Joe's picture of an ear.

Everyone laughed, except for his friends. They had been thinking about the ears, too.

By morning break, Andrew had come up with a theory.

"It must be a lab where they study dead bodies and what they died from," he suggested. "My cousin is a doctor. He had to study dead bodies at college. He had to cut them up and stuff."

"They were talking about someone aging," Roy reminded them. "It can't be just dead people in there."

"There's only one way to find out," Joe said. "We will have to go back in tonight."

The bunker lid came up easily this time. The boys were soon inside, creeping along the hallways.

"We could try the basement," Andrew whispered. "They have to keep the dead bodies somewhere."

Roy made a face.

"Why don't we just look in the lab with the trays and stuff?" he said.

Joe was already sliding down the stair railing, into the basement. The others were about to follow when they heard a rumbling noise.

Joe hid as a giant cart came toward him.

Then he signaled that the way was clear.

"It said 'Clinical Waste' on the side," he told the others. "Roy must be right. It's some sort of hospital."

"Clinical waste could be . . . ," Andrew fell silent. They could hear a strange noise. It sounded like animals, but it couldn't be.

Joe led the others along the hallway and stopped by a door. He slipped through it.

There was the sweet smell of warm hay. Something pushed against Joe's leg. He put his hand out and felt in the dark. His fingers sank into thick wool.

They were in a pen of sheep.

CHAPTER 5

The Freezer

"Anybody have a flashlight?" Joe asked.

Roy felt in his pocket. "Here."

Joe shined the light around the pen. There were fifty or sixty sheep. Joe swung the light around. The pool of light shined on faces, legs, and tails.

"They're all the same," he whispered.

"Sheep usually are," Roy said flatly.

"That's why you count them when you are trying to sleep," he added.

"No, look." Joe shined the light for the others.

The sheep were all exactly the same size and color. They had black markings on their faces and legs, in exactly the same places.

"They are clones," Joe said slowly. "I'm sure of it. They are identical."

"I just stepped in something," Roy said. "Can we get out of here?"

"Okay, we'll take another look at the lab upstairs," Joe agreed. "Those trays had labels."

The labels were not much help. They were just a jumble of letters and numbers.

"What's this?" Doug had found a freezer. He opened the lid and some cold white smoke escaped.

"You don't think there are frozen heads in there, do you?" Roy said.

"They don't do head transplants," Joe said. "Although it wouldn't be a bad idea for Roy."

"No," Roy said, "but some people have their heads frozen, so they can be brought back to life in the future. I read about it in science class."

"They're not heads," Joe said. "They might be eggs. They keep them frozen, and make babies out of them."

Just then, they heard a dog barking. It was time to get out.

"I read some stuff about cloning," Joe said. They were searching for clues on the Internet at Joe's house.

"Yeah, but they've already done that somewhere else," Andrew said. "Don't you remember Dolly the Sheep? Why should it be so secret if that's all they're doing?"

Joe shook his head. "That's what we're going to find out."

Later that night, Joe was climbing up the ladder from the bunker when he heard footsteps.

A woman in a white coat walked past. She slid open a window and checked inside one of the rooms.

She wrote something down on a pad, shut the window, and got into the elevator.

"Let's see what's in that room," Joe whispered.

They slid open the window.

"It's puppies," Joe said. "Hundreds of them."

They peered in at the sleeping puppies. They were all identical.

Then one of the puppies opened its eyes.

It began barking. The others began barking, too. The noise was incredible.

"We'd better get out of here," Joe said. Suddenly, a security guard and his dog burst out of the elevator.

"Hurry!" Joe said as they ran for the bunker.

They hurtled down the ladder one by one.

In the darkness, Joe heard a yell. It sounded like Roy.

They stood panting outside the
bunker entrance.

"Where's Roy?" Joe said.

"He was behind me," Doug said.

"Let's think. Maybe he's hiding,"
Joe said. "I say we wait a few minutes.
Then we go back in and rescue him."

"If they got him, they'll take him to
the police," Andrew said. He pointed at
the sign on the gate.

27

"We'll keep a watch on the gates," Joe said. "Then we'll know."

It was getting late. There was still no sign of Roy.

Nothing had come in or out of the gates.

"I think we should go back in," Joe said at last. "He might be locked up or something."

The others looked scared.

"What's the worst they can do to us?" Joe said. "We can say we found the bunker by accident, and didn't know it was private property."

Joe was the first one through the bunker, but it was Andrew who spotted the blood. A red trail led along the hallway.

"He must have fallen and hurt himself," Joe said. The trail led them to a room at the end of the hallway. Silently, Joe opened the door.

They stood amazed. Roy was lying on a bed, propped up by cushions. He was eating ice cream and watching television.

His head and leg were bandaged.

"Hi, everybody!" he grinned.

"What happened to you?" Joe asked, with a glance at the door behind him.

"I fell down the ladder and hit my head," Roy said. "I must have cut my leg, too. It really hurts. I just woke up here."

"Who gave you the food?" asked Andrew.

"Don't know. It was just here. I'm watching television," said Roy.

"We've got to get you out of here," Joe growled. "Can you walk?"

"I think so."

Roy swung his legs out of bed. It hurt a little, but he was still able to stand up.

"Okay, let's go," said Roy.

CHAPTER 8
Face to Face

Roy's head healed quickly. His leg took longer. Under the bandage, he had a long scar.

"So, you really don't remember anything?" Joe asked.

Roy shook his head.

"You had a lucky escape. We all did," Joe said.

The Reactor really was off limits now. It was just too dangerous.

Roy knew the people in there had taken care of him. Perhaps if he got back in, just one more time, he could find out what was really going on.

One night, Roy went back alone. He found the room where they had nursed him. A night light was on.

There was someone on the bed. It was a boy, about Roy's age. He had dark hair like Roy. He was sleeping.

Roy stood frozen in the doorway. He opened his mouth to scream, but nothing came out.

Then his clone opened its eyes and stared back at him.

About the Author

Jillian Powell started writing when she was very young. She loved having a giant pad of paper and some pens or crayons in front of her. She made up newspaper stories about jewel thieves and spies. Jillian's parents still have her early stories, complete with crayon illustrations!

About the Illustrator

Paul Savage works in a design studio. He says illustrating books is "the best job." He's always been interested in illustrating books, and he loves reading. Paul also enjoys playing sports and running.

He lives in England with his wife and his daughter, Amelia.

Glossary

clinical waste (KLIN-ik-uhl WAYST)—garbage or trash from a hospital or medical building

clone (KLOHN)—an identical copy of another animal or person

hurtled (HUR-tuhld)—moved with great speed

laboratory (LAB-rah-tor-ee)—a room or building with special tools and machines for doing scientific experiments and tests

pen (PEN)—an enclosed area or room where animals are kept

specimen (SPESS-uh-mun)—plants, animals, or humans, or parts of them, that are used in scientific experiments

theory (THEER-ee)—an idea that explains how or why something happened

Discussion Questions

1. Should animals be cloned? Should be people be cloned? Why or why not?

2. What really did happen to Roy? Explain how you know. Are there clues in the story that tell you?

3. Do you think Roy should tell anyone about what he saw at the end of the story? Why or why not?

Writing Prompts

1. Re-read page 24. With your teacher's or librarians's help, find a website about cloning. Find out more information. What did you learn? What do you think about it? Write about it.

2. Why are scientists interested in making clones?

3. Will the boys go back to the Reactor? Write about what might happen if they do.

Also by J. Powell

Big Brother at School

The newly installed security cameras in the classrooms and a special "health check" day have made Lee suspicious. He is determined to stop his principal's mysterious plan before it is too late!

Code Breakers

Brad, Conor, and Scott are bored — until they find the briefcase. When they discover a cell phone number, it leads them from clue to clue and eventually to a cold, damp cave. What is at the end of the trail?

Other Books in This Set

Summer Trouble
by Jonny Zucker

Tom's summer plans change when his cousin decides to visit. He believes his entire vacation will be ruined until Ben comes to his rescue in a rough situation.

Race of a Lifetime
by Tony Norman

Jamie's chances of winning the school bike race look good after he buys a new bike. Unfortunately, he runs into trouble before the race even begins.

Internet Sites

Do you want to know more about subjects related to this book? Or are you interested in learning about other topics? Then check out FactHound, a fun, easy way to find Internet sites.

Our investigative staff has already sniffed out great sites for you!

Here's how to use FactHound:

1. Visit *www.facthound.com*

2. Select your grade level.

3. To learn more about subjects related to this book, type in the book's ISBN number: **1598890948**.

4. Click the **Fetch It** button.

FactHound will fetch the best Internet sites for you!